Keisha to the
Rescue
Reed, Teresa
AR Quiz No. 14679 EN

AR Points: 2.0
Book Level: 4.9
Lexile Level: 800
Word Count: 10116

KEISHA TO THE RESCUE

by Teresa Reed

Illustrations by
Dan Burr

Spot Illustrations by
Rich Grote and Catherine Huerta

MAGIC ATTIC PRESS

Betsy Gould, Publisher
Marva Martin, Art Director
Robin Haywood, Managing Editor

Edited by Laurie Orseck
Designed by Susi Oberhelman

ISBN 1-57513-070-X

As members of the
MAGIC ATTIC CLUB,
we promise to
be best friends,
share all of our adventures in the attic,
use our imaginations,
have lots of fun together,
and remember—the real magic is in us.

Alison   *Keisha*

Heather   *Megan*

Contents

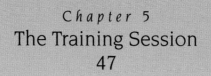

AN ERRAND
FOR ELLIE

 eisha Vance waved as she headed toward the corner where her three best friends stood waiting. "Sorry I'm late," she called. "My aunt Dionne was over, and she—"

"Wow," Alison McCann said before Keisha could finish. "Your hair looks great."

"Thanks." Keisha grinned, then twirled round and round so her friends could see the rows of tightly woven, beaded braids in her long dark hair. "I like it, too."

"Did you do it yourself?" asked Heather Hardin.

"Are you kidding?" Keisha shook her head. "My aunt did it for me. It took a long time—that's why I'm late," she added apologetically. "Have you guys been waiting awhile?"

"We just got here a few minutes ago," Megan Ryder explained. "We stopped at Ellie's first so that we could pick up her prescription."

"We have to bring it to the pharmacy in Oakview," Alison chimed in. "The one in town is out of the pain medicine Ellie needs."

"We'd better get going," Megan reminded them. "It's almost three o'clock, and I have to be home by dinnertime."

"Poor Ellie," Keisha said as the girls began walking the short distance to the neighboring town of Oakview. "I remember when I sprained *my* ankle. It hurt a lot."

Megan nodded. "It's going to be hard for Ellie to manage by herself while she's on crutches for two weeks."

"She's not going to manage by herself," Alison reminded them. "She's got the Magic Attic Club to help her out."

"That's right," Keisha agreed. "Ellie's done so many

8

nice things for us—it's our turn to help her out."

Ellie Goodwin lived near the girls and was their close friend. They all thought Ellie was one of the most interesting women they'd ever met. Ellie's career had taken her all over the world, and the attic of her white Victorian house was crammed with objects she'd collected on her trips—books, letters, boxes, and framed photos of all sorts of places and people.

But Keisha and her friends considered the old steamer truck in Ellie's attic the most amazing object of all. It was filled with unusual clothing and accessories. Whenever the girls tried on one of the outfits from the trunk and stood in front of the tall, gilt-edged mirror beside it, they found themselves transported to a different place and time. Shortly after they discovered the secret of Ellie's attic, they decided to form their own club, the Magic Attic Club.

The girls were still talking about Ellie's sprained ankle as they turned down the main street that wound through Oakview. Keisha gazed around at the rows of quaint homes and attractive boutiques. There was a toy shop with a huge teddy bear in the window, a health food store, and a café, where several people sat outside reading papers and sipping coffee.

"I hope those people don't get wet," Alison said,

holding up the big golf umbrella she was carrying. "My dad made me take this—it's supposed to rain later."

"There it is," Megan said suddenly, pointing across the street.

Keisha looked up. Megan was pointing to a small store under a red awning. The sign out front read OAKVIEW DRUGS.

"Omigosh!" Alison gasped suddenly. "I can't believe it!"

Keisha turned to see what her friend was talking about.

Alison was staring at a two-story, brick bookstore with dark green shutters across the street.

"This is incredible," Alison went on. "Maria Rodriguez is right here in Oakview, inside that bookstore!"

"Maria Rodriguez?" Heather wrinkled her nose. "Who's that?"

Keisha was about to ask the same question. Then she noticed the big placard on the sidewalk in front of the store: MEET OLYMPIC GOLD MEDALIST MARIA RODRIGUEZ TODAY, FROM 2 TO 4 PM. SHE WILL BE AUTOGRAPHING COPIES OF HER NEW BEST-SELLER, RACING LIKE THE WIND.

"Isn't she that Olympic sprinter?" Megan asked. "The one who won all those medals a few years ago?"

"I thought she was a pole-vaulter," Heather said.

"I can't believe you guys don't know who she is!" Alison declared, putting her hands on her hips. "For your information, Maria Rodriguez holds the world record in speed skating. At the last winter Olympics, she won two gold medals."

Keisha, Heather, and Megan exchanged grins. Alison liked almost all sports, but she especially loved figure skating and speed skating. It sometimes took her by surprise that her friends weren't as enthusiastic as she was.

"I'd love to meet her," Alison murmured as she went over to the front door of the bookstore and peered inside.

"So let's go," Heather said.

"We don't have time," Alison replied. When she turned around to face her friends again, her blue eyes were filled with disappointment. "The line is too long."

"Tell you what, Alison," Keisha offered. "I'll go get Ellie's prescription while you guys go into the bookstore. I'll meet you back here in a little while."

"Really?" Alison said, her expression brightening.

"Sure," Keisha replied. "You may find this hard to believe," she added with a smile, "but I'm not really that interested in meeting Maria Rodriguez."

"You're the best, Keisha," Alison declared, smiling

back. "When somebody offers me a million dollars for Maria's autograph, I'll split the money with you, I promise!"

"It's a deal," Keisha replied, laughing.

"Here you go." Heather handed Keisha a small slip of paper with scribbled handwriting. "This is Ellie's prescription."

"Okay," Keisha replied. "I'll see you guys in a few minutes." She watched her three friends hurry into the bookstore, then headed across the street. As she pushed open the door to Oakview Drugs, a bell above her head jangled. She looked around for the prescription counter and found a sign that pointed to the rear of the store. As Keisha made her way past displays filled with potpourri, the store's wide, wooden floorboards creaked under her feet.

A bald man wearing glasses, a white lab coat, and a nametag that read YOUR PHARMACIST MR. BURNS, stood behind the counter.

"What did you say?" an older man asked the pharmacist. "Do I take this once a day, or twice a day?"

Keisha flashed the pharmacist a sympathetic smile: he'd just finished telling the man he was supposed to take the medicine twice a day.

Mr. Burns didn't smile back. Instead he gave her a cold look, then turned back to the man and began explaining all over again how the medicine worked.

Keisha flushed. She was just trying to be friendly—why had the pharmacist reacted like that?

A woman standing behind Keisha began sighing and tapping her foot nervously. Keisha felt impatient, too, but she tried not to let it show. She tried to occupy herself by gazing around at all the items in the small drugstore. Several flavors of herbal cough drops were arranged in neat rows along the counter. Next to them were bars of English soaps in pretty pastel wrappers and bottles of expensive hand lotion.

Then something else sitting on the counter caught Keisha's eye: a tall display of colorful bracelets.

Keisha glanced back at Mr. Burns. He was still deep in conversation with the older man, so Keisha moved closer to the display to get a better look. The bracelets were woven with brightly colored thread and beads. A purple one with an intricate pattern running through it especially caught her eye.

If I can find four matching bracelets, she thought, I can buy one for myself and one for Megan, Alison, and Heather.

Keisha checked the counter again. The older man had finally left, but now Mr. Burns was helping the woman who'd been behind Keisha.

Oh well, Keisha thought. I don't mind missing my turn. She spun the rack around several times but she could find only three purple bracelets. There were four green ones, so she took one down and began to fasten it around her wrist.

It wasn't as pretty as the purple one, but maybe—

"Don't touch those bracelets unless you plan to buy one!" a voice said sharply.

Keisha was so startled that the green bracelet slid from her wrist. When she looked up, she saw Mr. Burns staring in her direction, an angry scowl on his face.

"Excuse me?" Keisha said, feeling her face flush.

"I said, don't touch those bracelets unless you're planning to buy one, young lady," Mr. Burns repeated. "There are security cameras all over the store."

Keisha's face burned.

The realization hit her like a ton of bricks. Mr. Burns was accusing her of stealing.

Chapter

Two

ACCUSED!

eisha couldn't believe it. She had never stolen anything in her life. How dare Mr. Burns accuse her! She wanted to explain what had happened, but for a moment she was too stunned to speak, or even move.

In a daze, Keisha bent down to pick up the bracelet that had fallen to the floor. Calm down, she told herself as she hung it back on the rack. It's okay. But her fingers were trembling, and her face still felt as if it were on fire. She had only been looking at the bracelets—

why would the pharmacist accuse her of stealing?

But Keisha already knew the answer. It was because she was African-American.

Keisha remembered the last time someone had been suspicious because of the color of her skin. The year before, while her family was visiting her mother's friend from college, two policemen had pulled over their car. Her father later explained to her that the policemen weren't used to seeing black people in their town, but the incident made him angry. When they saw the Vances, they'd immediately become suspicious. That was exactly how Keisha felt now: angry and ashamed.

Leave the store, commanded a voice inside Keisha's head. But she knew she couldn't. Ellie needed the medicine for her ankle. No matter how angry Keisha was, the last thing she wanted to do was let Ellie down.

Slowly, Keisha approached the counter again. When it was her turn, she slid the small slip of paper with Ellie's prescription on it across the counter without a word.

Mr. Burns didn't even look at it—or at Keisha. "Sorry," he said in a cold voice. "I don't dispense medicine to minors."

"But my friend needs this," Keisha began. "I'm sure if you call her, she'll tell you—"

"Next," Mr. Burns called out. A man who'd come up behind Keisha stepped up to the counter before she

could get out another word.

With trembling fingers, Keisha reached for Ellie's prescription. She scooped it up, then whirled around and raced for the door so she could escape to the street.

Everything was a blur as Keisha rushed along the sidewalk toward the bookstore where she'd left her friends. Each time the scene in the drugstore played over in her mind, she felt another flush of anger and embarrassment.

How could Mr. Burns treat her like that? It was so unfair. No matter what he said, Keisha didn't believe for a minute that her age was the reason he wouldn't give her the medicine. He simply didn't want her in his store because she was an African-American.

Angry tears spilled down her cheeks. Keisha was so upset, she didn't notice three friendly faces coming toward her.

"Hey, Keisha!" Alison yelled, waving a rolled-up poster. "Wait till you see what Maria Rodriguez gave me! It's a really cool picture, and she . . ."

Alison's words trailed off as she drew closer.

"Omigosh, Keisha," she said. "What's wrong?"

"Are you okay?" Heather asked, her brown eyes filled with worry.

"No," Keisha said, shaking her head. "That man is a racist," she blurted out. "He doesn't like black people."

Keisha told her friends what had happened in the drugstore.

"Are you sure it was because you're black?" Alison asked. "Maybe Mr. Burns really didn't want to give you the prescription because you're a kid."

"That's probably why he thought you were shoplifting, too," Megan chimed in.

"Right," Heather said. "Maybe we can all go back in there together and ask him to call Ellie."

"No way," Keisha said fiercely. "I'm never, ever going back inside that place!" She thrust the prescription into Heather's hand, then stomped over to a bench near the curb and sat down.

Her three friends exchanged looks.

"What should we do?" Alison whispered. "We have to get Ellie's medicine."

"I'll go to the pharmacy," Megan offered quietly.

"Maybe I can talk him into giving it to me—even though I'm a minor."

"That's a good idea," Heather agreed. "I'll come with you. Alison, why don't you stay with Keisha."

Alison nodded, and went over to sit down next to Keisha. Ten minutes later, Heather and Megan were back.

Keisha's eyes immediately flicked to Megan. In her friend's hand was a small white package.

"I told you!" Keisha said as fresh tears sprung into her eyes.

"I'm sorry, Keisha," Megan said in a choked voice. "I didn't think . . ." She couldn't finish her sentence. Tears had welled up in her eyes, too.

Keisha turned away and pulled a tissue out of her pocket. She knew her friends felt bad for her, but it didn't matter. They couldn't know how she really felt.

As Keisha stood up, it began to rain. The four girls huddled together under Mr. McCann's golf umbrella and began to head back to Ellie's house.

But for the first time Keisha could remember since she'd known her friends, she felt completely alone.

The girls found Ellie on the sofa in her sitting room, with her swollen ankle propped up on several pillows. She was wearing a comfortable-looking gray sweatsuit, and a stack of books was piled up next to her. Classical music played softly in the background.

None of the girls wanted to talk about what had happened at Oakview Drugs, but when Ellie asked what had taken them so long, they didn't have a choice. Megan quickly told her about Mr. Burns, an embarrassed look on her face the whole time.

As Ellie listened, her normally bright blue eyes clouded over. She didn't say a word until Megan was finished. When she did finally speak, her voice sounded tight and angry. "I've met a lot of people in my lifetime," she said. "And you know what? It still surprises me how ignorant some of them can be." Her eyes traveled slowly to Keisha. "In my opinion, folks like Mr. Burns need to be told to their faces how shamefully they've acted."

Keisha could feel Ellie's eyes on her, but she kept her own eyes pinned to the floor as she went on petting Monty, Ellie's West Highland terrier. She didn't want to look at anyone, or even talk about what had happened. All she wanted to do was forget the whole scene.

Finally, to Keisha's relief, the conversation turned to Ellie's sprained ankle.

"We'll come back tomorrow, in case you need anything, Ellie," Heather said.

"You girls have already brought me everything," Ellie declared. "Thanks to you, I have enough casseroles to last a week, plus five library books to read. What else could an old woman with a sprained ankle want?"

"How about an un-sprained ankle?" Alison joked.

"You're right," Ellie said with a laugh. "That is something I could use."

Keisha was about to follow her friends to the front door.

"Keisha?" Ellie called out gently.

Keisha turned around. "Yes?"

"I hate to be a burden." Ellie gave an embarrassed little laugh. "But I just realized that I do need something else. Can you stay and help me make dinner?"

Surprised, Keisha stared at Ellie for a second. Finally she shrugged. "Sure," she said. "I'll stay, as long as my mom says it's okay."

Keisha said good-bye to her friends, then reached for the phone.

When Keisha hung up with her mother a short while later, Ellie was nowhere to be seen.

"Ellie?" Keisha called.

"I'm in here," Ellie replied from the kitchen.

As Keisha entered Ellie's large kitchen, she couldn't

believe her eyes. The kitchen table was set, a salad was made, and two plates of lasagna sat near the microwave oven, ready to be warmed up.

"Ellie!" Keisha accused her. "You made the whole thing up. You don't need my help!"

Ellie's blue eyes were twinkling. "Guilty as charged," she confessed. "But it was for a good cause." Then she hobbled over to Keisha on her crutches. "I thought you might need some time in the attic," she added, reaching out to touch Keisha's long, beaded braids.

"That's a great idea!" She hesitated one more second. "Are you sure you don't need my help?"

Ellie shook her head.

"Thanks," Keisha replied, giving the older woman a kiss on the cheek. Then she hurried toward the small table near the front door and opened the silver box where Ellie kept the key to the attic. Keisha held it tightly as she ran up the stairs.

As soon as she entered the attic and shut the door, Keisha could feel her whole body relax. It was so quiet and peaceful there. The only sound was the rain outside as it pelted the roof. Ellie was right, she thought. I do need to be alone for awhile.

Keisha reached for the satin pull cord on the hanging lamp. Then she crossed the worn oriental rug and headed for the sturdy steamer trunk that sat on the floor.

As Keisha knelt beside the black leather and oak trunk, a thrill went through her. The trunk was filled with amazing outfits, each holding the promise of an exciting adventure.

Keisha rummaged through the trunk, trying to choose an outfit. Then something caught her eye.

"Look at this," she murmured as she pulled out a garment splashed with fuchsia, purple, and green. "It's a swimsuit."

It had been such a dreary, rainy day—suddenly the thought of swimming in a warm place lifted Keisha's spirits.

She reached back into the trunk and found a matching windbreaker, as well as a beach bag packed with a towel, sunglasses, and sunscreen. Quickly, Keisha pulled on the brightly colored outfit, then lifted the beach bag onto her shoulder. Next she hurried over to look at herself in the tall, gilt-edged mirror that stood near the trunk.

An instant later, the walls of Ellie's attic had disappeared.

Keisha smiled with delight when she saw what had replaced them. Over her head stretched a bright blue, cloudless sky. At her feet lay a beautiful swimming pool, shimmering in the sunlight.

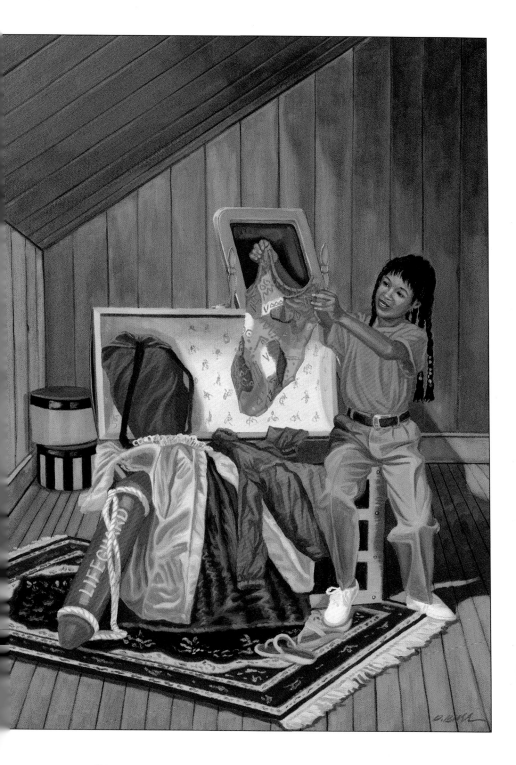

C h a p t e r

Three

KEISHA
DIVES IN

ow listen up, everybody!" A young woman wearing a windbreaker suddenly clapped her hands. She held a clipboard in her hands as she introduced herself to a group of swimmers standing around the pool. "I'm Coach Owen. Welcome to your first day as a lifeguard at Brookside Country Club."

I'm a lifeguard at Brookside Country Club? Keisha thought as she gazed around. This was a beautiful place—what a great setting for an adventure!

The large pool in front of her had a shallow section near where Keisha was standing and a deeper section, with a diving board, at the opposite end. Beyond the pool Keisha could see a golf course in the distance, with lush green grass and gently rolling hills, and several tennis courts. Out near the parking lot, colorful flowerbeds and rows of neatly trimmed hedges seemed to close off Brookside from the rest of the world.

Suddenly Keisha realized she'd better pay attention to what the coach was saying. She was a good swimmer, but she'd never been a lifeguard before. She didn't want to miss anything important.

"Some of you, like Lisette, worked here last year," Coach Owen was saying, smiling at a red-haired girl, "so you know the ropes. But most of our staff is new, so I'm going to be going over everything very carefully."

Keisha listened as Coach Owen reviewed some of the more important rules at the pool: no running, no splashing, no glass bottles.

"I've posted the work schedule outside the locker room," the coach went on. "Be sure to check it every week so you know when your shifts are and when you'll be giving swimming lessons."

The redhead named Lisette groaned. "We have to teach swimming, too? Is it all work and no play around here?"

"Don't worry, Lisette," Coach Owen replied. "Once in awhile we'll have some fun. Just like last year, there's a barbecue for the lifeguards every Friday night. Our first one is tomorrow," she added.

Everyone cheered at that. To Keisha, everything sounded like fun—even giving swimming lessons.

"Do we get to train every day?" a girl asked. She had brown hair pulled back in a short ponytail and green eyes, and was about Keisha's age. But she was wearing a washed-out, blue bathing suit instead of the brightly colored swimsuit all the other lifeguards had on.

"Yes, Morgan." Coach Owen nodded. "And that's exactly what we're going to do right now," she added, pointing to the deep section. "Twenty laps, everybody!"

As Keisha made her way to the far side of the pool she noticed the coach talking in low tones to Morgan. Morgan had her head down, and her cheeks looked flushed, as if she was embarrassed about something.

Keisha got on one of the two lines that had been formed and watched as the first two lifeguards dove in. They both looked like strong swimmers; she hoped

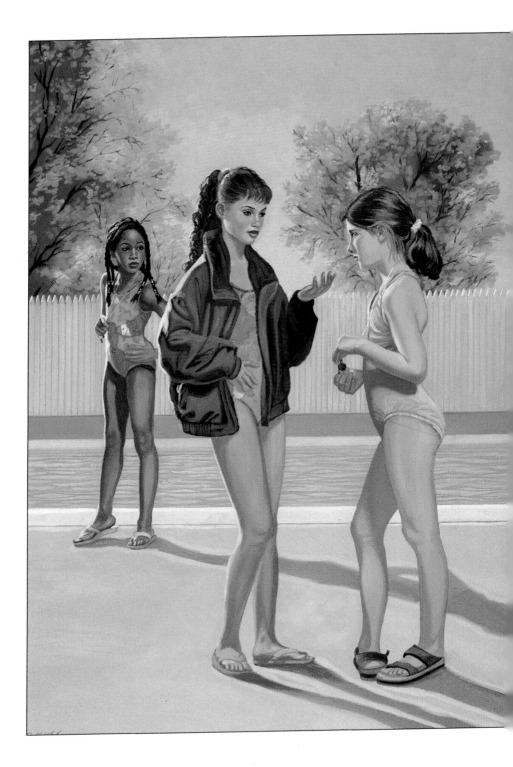

she could swim just as well when it was her turn.

Suddenly someone tapped her on the shoulder.

It was Lisette. "You're new this year, right?" she asked, giving Keisha a friendly smile. "I heard you're one of the lifeguards staying at the bungalow with the coach for the summer."

Keisha nodded, pretending she knew exactly what was going on.

"You're going to love it there," Lisette went on. "My friend Tanya is staying there for the summer, too, and she says it's a blast. It's got a kitchen and everything."

A minute later Morgan came over and stood on the other line. Keisha couldn't help noticing that her cheeks were still flushed and there was a worried expression in her eyes.

"Are you okay?" Keisha asked.

Morgan shook her head. She hesitated for a second, then blurted out, "Actually I'm pretty upset. The coach just told me I have to buy two lifeguard swimsuits by this weekend. If I don't have them, they'll kick me off the squad."

"Are you busy this weekend or something?" Keisha asked.

"No, that's not it." Morgan looked uncomfortable. "I can't afford to buy them until we get our first paycheck," she admitted. "I knew I would need the swimsuits when they hired me," she went on, "but I didn't think it would be such a big deal."

Lisette had been listening to the conversation. "This isn't the community pool, Morgan Reilly," she snapped.

Keisha was surprised by how sharply Lisette had spoken to Morgan.

"The members of Brookside pay a lot to belong here, you know," Lisette went on. "They expect the lifeguards to look professional. And how do you expect people to know you're a lifeguard if you're not wearing the right swimsuit?"

"I know." Morgan nodded. "It's important for the swimmers to be able to tell who's a lifeguard. It's just that I can't afford to buy the swimsuits yet," she repeated.

"Can't your parents afford to buy them for you?" Lisette asked.

"No," Morgan said, sounding a little annoyed. "I'm sure you know they can't, Lisette."

At that moment the boy ahead of Morgan dove into the pool and started his laps. Morgan waited till he was halfway down the lane, then dove in after him.

"Poor Morgan," Keisha said. "That sounds like a hard situation."

Lisette shrugged. "I don't feel sorry for her," she

said. "Actually, I'm surprised the coach hired her in the first place."

"Why?" Keisha asked, glancing toward the water, where Morgan was doing the butterfly stroke. "She looks like a great swimmer."

"Morgan *is* a great swimmer," a girl nearby chimed in. She had short black hair and dark eyes. "I don't know why you give her such a hard time, Lisette. Just because her father—"

"Come on, Tanya," Lisette interrupted. "Morgan doesn't really belong at Brookside."

Keisha was about to ask Lisette what she meant. But the lifeguard on line ahead of her was already halfway down the lane. It was Keisha's turn to start her laps.

Keisha stretched out her arms and dove neatly into the pool. As she glided through the clear blue water, she forgot all about what Lisette had said. All she could think about was how great it felt to be there, in the pool, far away from home and what had happened in Mr. Burns's pharmacy.

Chapter

Four

ON DUTY

ater that afternoon, Keisha climbed into the lifeguard chair at the shallow end of the pool. She adjusted the umbrella over her chair to block out the sun, and put down her beach towel so she wouldn't have to sit directly on the hot seat.

"Hi Keisha!" Morgan waved and smiled from across the pool, where she and Lisette were on duty at the deep end. "Good luck on your first shift."

"Thanks," Keisha replied, smiling back. "I think I'm ready."

Morgan gave her a thumbs-up, then turned back to her end to blow her whistle at some kids who were acting rowdy on the diving board.

Keisha quickly got settled for her first shift. She checked the lifeguard chair to make sure the rescue buoy was hanging there and that the first-aid kit was in the compartment 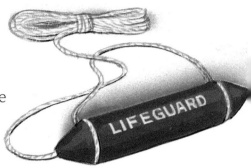 under her seat. She certainly hoped she wouldn't have any emergencies while she was on duty, but it was good to know that the equipment was in place—just in case.

Finally Keisha was ready to get to work. Her end of the pool was crowded with parents and little children who were squealing happily as they splashed around in the water. A group of older women stood in the pool near the steps, laughing loudly at something one of them in a flowered bathing cap was saying.

Keisha kept focused on the swimmers at her end, occasionally checking the deep end as well. Coach Owen had emphasized that it was important to keep an eye on the whole pool.

Keisha could already tell that it was harder to be on duty at the deep end. That was where the older kids hung

out, and Morgan had already blown her whistle several
times to warn them to stop fooling around. She seemed
to have everything under control, but to Keisha's
surprise, Lisette didn't appear to be helping out at all.
All she was doing was joking around with her friends—
especially a dark-haired, athletic-looking boy Keisha
had met earlier named Brandon.

"Watch it there, boys!"

A loud voice drew Keisha's attention back to her
part of the pool. The woman in the flowered bathing cap
looked furious as she yelled at some teenagers, "You're
splashing everybody!"

It was Brandon and his friends, who had moved down
to her area, where they were playing Marco Polo and
annoying practically everyone in the shallow area.

Keisha stood up and gave a short blast on her whistle.

"No splashing," she called out.

Brandon turned to look at her. For a second, Keisha
expected him to say something nasty
back to her.

Instead, he smiled.
"Okay, Lifeguard," he
said, giving her a salute.
"We're out of here anyway. It's
too shallow at this end."

Keisha felt relieved as Brandon and his friends headed back toward the diving board. That was the first time she had blown her whistle, and she'd been a little worried that the boys wouldn't listen to her.

But, a few minutes later, they started acting up again—this time in the deep end. Brandon was bouncing up and down on the diving board while his friends stayed in the water below, taunting him to jump in.

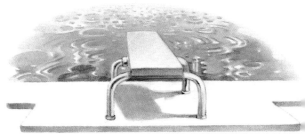

Brandon had better be careful, Keisha thought. It was dangerous to bounce like that on a slippery board.

Keisha looked in Lisette's direction, sure that she would warn him. But Lisette didn't seem the least bit worried. In fact, a few minutes later, she joined in the fun.

"What are you, chicken?" she teased Brandon. "Afraid to dive off?"

"Yeah," added one of the boys. "Let's see you do a jackknife, Brandon!"

Brandon grinned and started bouncing higher, making the board flap up and down.

"Hey!" Morgan cried suddenly. "No bouncing on the

board! If you guys don't stop fooling around, I'll have to kick you out of the pool."

"Oh really?" Brandon stopped jumping and gave Morgan a cold stare. "Who says?"

"Me," Morgan stated calmly.

"You?" Brandon scoffed. "Gimme a break."

His friends in the water started laughing."Watch out, Brandon," one of them said. "When her daddy's finished cleaning the toilets, he's going to beat you up!"

Morgan held her whistle up to her face. "Jump in now, Brandon," she said. "Or you're out of the pool."

Keisha took off her sunglasses and watched along with everyone else in the pool as Brandon deliberately began to bounce up and down on the board again.

Morgan reacted in a flash. She shot to her feet, then blew on her whistle—hard. "That's it! Out of the pool for the rest of the day, Brandon!"

In an instant, Lisette was on her feet, too. "What do you think you're doing, Morgan?" she called out in an angry voice. "You can't kick him out!"

"I'm the lifeguard on duty," Morgan shot back, her green eyes flashing. "You may not like it, Lisette, but I have every right to tell Brandon what to do."

Just then Coach Owen strode over from the kiddie pool. "What's the problem?" she demanded.

Morgan filled her in, and the coach looked up at Brandon, who was still standing on the edge of the diving board. "You're out of the pool for the day," she called.

"Why?" he demanded. "I didn't do anything."

"Yes, you did," Coach Owen snapped back. "You weren't paying attention to the rules, or to Morgan's warning."

Lisette muttered something under her breath as Brandon turned around and stomped off.

Morgan sat down on her chair, nervously spinning the cord from her whistle around her finger. Keisha could tell that she was upset, but Keisha was impressed—it took guts to kick somebody out of the pool, especially with so many people watching.

I hope I do just as good a job when it's my turn to take charge at the pool, Keisha thought.

At five o'clock, Keisha's first shift was over. When Tyler, another lifeguard, came over to relieve her, she jumped down and headed for the locker room. On her way, Keisha realized how much she'd enjoyed her first day on the job.

Just then Keisha spotted Morgan near the tennis courts, and she hurried to catch up with her.

"You did a great job," Keisha told her. "It was really cool the way you dealt with Brandon."

"Thanks," Morgan said, giving her a grateful smile. "That's one thing I don't like about being a lifeguard," she confessed. "Enforcing the rules."

"It would have been a lot easier if Lisette had backed you up," Keisha said. "I don't want to put her down or anything," she added quickly. "I just thought we were supposed to help each other out in situations like that."

"That's what we're supposed to do," Morgan agreed. "But . . ." She let her words trail off, then shrugged. "I know Lisette from school, and that's the way she always treats me," she explained. "Lisette thinks she's better than me because her family's rich." Suddenly Morgan stopped talking. "Here she comes now," she said under her breath.

"Hi, Keisha!" Lisette called as she approached the two girls. She didn't even glance in Morgan's direction. "I've been looking all over for you, Keisha," she said. "I wanted to invite you to hang out with me and my friends at the barbecue tomorrow night. It'll be really fun."

A flush of embarrassment crossed Keisha's face. She couldn't understand why Lisette was including her and obviously leaving Morgan out.

"I've got to go," Morgan said suddenly. "My dad's driving me home. See you later, Keisha. Bye, Lisette."

Keisha waved good-bye, but Lisette turned her back.

"I can't believe that girl kicked Brandon out of the pool," Lisette said in an angry tone.

"I think she handled the situation well," Keisha said, sticking up for Morgan. "Brandon and his friends were acting like jerks."

Lisette rolled her eyes but dropped the subject. "Why don't you meet me right here before the barbecue tomorrow night," she went on. "That way we can grab the best table and sit together. See you tomorrow," she added before Keisha could get a word in.

Keisha was on her way into the locker room when she passed the hot tub. A red-haired woman who looked just like Lisette was shaking her finger at a maintenance man dressed in a green uniform.

"It's absolutely unacceptable," she was saying. "I don't know what you were thinking, Peter, but the temperature in that hot tub is about twenty degrees too cold. In all my years as a member here, I have never, ever . . ."

Keisha couldn't help feeling sorry for him as the woman went on and on.

"I'm sorry, Mrs. Wilson," he said. "I'll fix it right away."

"Come on, Dad," called a girl's voice from another direction. "We're late for dinner."

Keisha instantly recognized Morgan's voice.

"I'm coming, honey," the maintenance man replied. Embarrassed, he offered Lisette's mother one more apology.

Keisha was stunned. So *this* was Lisette's problem with Morgan's father?

THE TRAINING SESSION

he next morning Keisha woke at five-thirty. To her surprise, Coach Owen and the three other lifeguards staying at the bungalow were already gone. Keisha quickly pulled on her swimsuit and windbreaker and packed up her beach bag. She ate a bowl of cereal, then hurried out the door. The coach had called a training session for six o'clock, and she didn't want to be late.

The air was damp, and a light fog hung over the grounds of the country club. As Keisha made her way across the dew-drenched grass, the sun was still rising, trying to burn its way through the gray sky.

Several of the other lifeguards were already hanging around the pool, waiting for the training session to start.

As Keisha dropped down on a lounge chair, she heard Tyler, one of the lifeguards, joking around with Morgan.

"I saw you riding your bike up the driveway when my mom dropped me off," he teased her. "You were pedaling so slowly I thought you were about ninety years old!"

Morgan grinned. "I was half asleep, Tyler. I'm not used to getting up at five in the morning, you know."

"You'd better get used to it," Tyler said. "Now that you're a lifeguard, you'll have to be here by six o'clock almost every day."

"Then I'm going to catch up on my sleep whenever I can," Morgan replied.

Keisha laughed along with Tyler as Morgan closed her eyes and pretended to snore. She was glad to see Morgan having fun. Maybe Lisette looked down on Morgan because her father worked as a maintenance man at the country club, but obviously none of the other lifeguards did. In fact, Lisette was the only one who seemed to give Mr. Reilly's job a second thought.

48

The Training Session

A few minutes later, Coach Owen joined the squad of lifeguards at the pool. "Morning, everybody," she said, holding a steaming cup of coffee. "I know it's a little chilly this morning, so we're not going to do our laps just yet. We're going to cardiopulmonary resuscitation, instead."

"As we all know, CPR is probably the most important procedure for you lifeguards to master," the coach went on. It's often the most immediate way we can keep a person alive when her heart has stopped pumping, and she's not breathing. I know all of you have taken a CPR course to get your certification as lifeguards, but I think it's important to go over the basic procedure."

The lifeguards gathered around the diving board, where the coach had placed several dummies. One was of an adult, one of a small child, and one of an infant. Using the dummies, Coach Owen reviewed how to administer CPR.

Keisha leaned in to watch. She had learned CPR the year before in school, but it had been awhile since she'd seen someone do it.

"Now I want you guys to try," the coach announced. "Let's form three lines, one at each dummy. You need to practice on each of them," she added. "As we've just discussed, the procedure is a little different for babies and small children than it is for adults."

Keisha took her place on line behind the child dummy.

Lisette and Tanya were working side-by-side, practicing the technique. But from the look of things, they weren't taking any of it very seriously.

"Do I really have to pinch this kid's nose first?" Lisette giggled. "That's so disgusting!"

"Make sure you have a tissue," Tanya added, giggling too. "Then after that, tilt her head back and put your mouth on hers."

"That's even worse than pinching her nose," Lisette said, making a face. "What if she has bad breath?"

The two of them broke into a fresh round of laughter, and this time Keisha couldn't help smiling a little, too. It did seem weird to pinch a dummy's nose, put your mouth over its mouth, and then start blowing air into it!

But Coach Owen was not amused. In fact, when she noticed Tanya and Lisette giggling, she was furious.

"Cut it out, you two," she snapped. "This is not something you can afford to take lightly—even if you've worked as lifeguards before. CPR is used in a life-or-death situation."

Lisette and Tanya nodded when Coach Owen was finished. But as soon as she turned her back, Lisette made a face. "Aye, aye, Captain," she whispered.

Tanya snickered, but this time Keisha didn't join in. She didn't want to miss anything else the coach said.

When the training session was over, Keisha headed for the locker room. According to the schedule, she was supposed to teach her first swimming lesson at nine that morning.

Keisha opened her locker and grabbed her whistle and beach bag inside. As she was closing the door, Morgan came in.

"Hi," Keisha called. "Where's your first shift today?"

"At the kiddie pool," Morgan answered. "Unless I get fired," she added. "Coach Owen gave me another warning about my bathing suit."

Keisha listened sympathetically, not sure what to say. Keisha's own father was a hospital administrator and her mother was a nurse. Sometimes Keisha didn't like the fact that her parents worked so much, but she never had to worry about her family's money situation, like Morgan. "I wish I could help," she said finally.

Morgan smiled. "That's okay, Keisha," she said. "I'll figure something out. Thanks for listening."

Keisha glanced at the clock and realized it was almost nine o'clock. "I have to go," she said.

"Good luck teaching your first lesson," Morgan said. "I

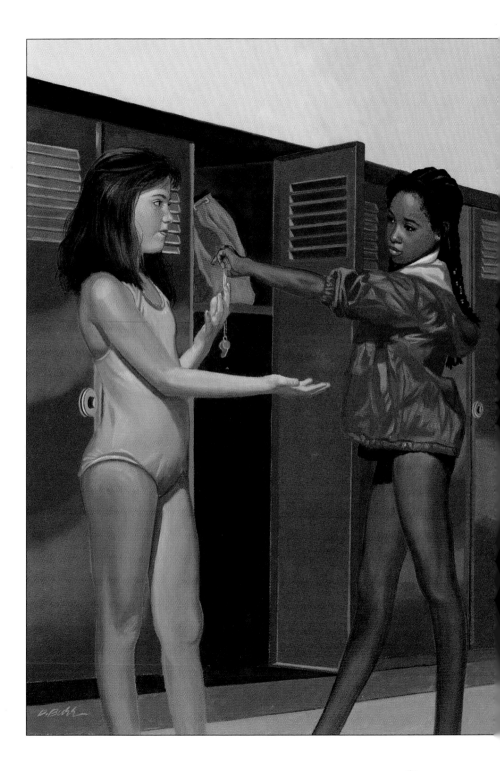

had my first class yesterday, and it was really fun."

"I can't wait," Keisha said, and on her way over to the pool, she realized it was true. She was really looking forward to teaching some of the younger kids how to swim.

"Great job, Mary," Keisha said. The little girl was holding onto a lifeguard buoy as she practiced kicking.

The blonde-haired toddler smiled happily at Keisha's praise. "It's fun," she said, kicking even harder and spraying Keisha in the face.

"Okay, that's enough!" Keisha said, laughing. She beckoned to the next student. Her class consisted of three four-year-olds, twins named Mary and Ryan and a little boy named Dylan.

"You're next, Dylan," Keisha said to the cute little boy with dark hair and tanned skin. "Want to try jumping in? I'll hold you, I promise."

"No." Dylan's dark eyes looked enormous as he shook his head back and forth. "I don't want to."

"Okay," Keisha said. She knew that if she pushed too hard, Dylan would never come back for his second lesson. He might even get more scared of the water.

A few minutes later, their time was up.

"Great job, guys," Keisha called as Mary and Ryan's father came to collect them.

"Where's my brother?" Dylan asked. "My mom said he was coming to pick me up."

Keisha had been thinking the same thing. Dylan's mother dropped him off for his lesson and said Dylan's brother would come to pick him up. But so far, nobody had shown up for the little boy. Dylan looked worried, and Keisha was getting worried, too. Her shift at the kiddie pool started in ten minutes.

Fifteen minutes later, a tall boy carrying a tennis racket strode over to the pool.

"How'd it go, little buddy?" he said to Dylan.

It took Keisha a moment to recognize Dylan's older brother. It was Lisette's friend, Brandon.

"Good," Dylan said. He took a flying leap at Brandon, and Brandon caught him in his arms.

"Sorry I'm late," Brandon said to Keisha.

Keisha nodded curtly. She was annoyed, but at least Brandon had finally shown up. "I'll see you soon, Dylan," she said. "You did a great job today."

Dylan smiled at Keisha. "I like your whistle," he said.

"Thanks," Keisha told him as she hurried over to the kiddie pool to start her shift.

"Oh, Keisha," Brandon called

after her. "I wanted to ask you a favor."

She spun around. "What is it?" she said impatiently. "I'm already late."

"I've got a couple of tennis matches this afternoon," Brandon began, "and I was wondering if you could watch Dylan for awhile."

For a second Keisha was speechless. She couldn't believe Brandon's nerve.

"Sorry, Brandon. You'll have to find somebody else," she said finally. "I'm on duty all afternoon. There's no way I can guard the pool and watch Dylan at the same time."

"Okay." Brandon shrugged. "Just thought I'd ask."

Keisha headed once again to the kiddie pool. Brandon's too much, she thought. First he shows up fifteen minutes late to pick up his brother. Then he has the nerve to ask me to baby-sit!

When Keisha reached the chair at the kiddie pool, the lifeguard on duty was looking at her watch.

"Sorry I'm late," Keisha called.

"That's okay," the girl said. "The kiddie pool's been empty all morning. It's been a piece of cake." She climbed down, and Keisha took the chair.

The pool was still empty, so Keisha spent the next few minutes getting settled and put her visor on. The view from the lifeguard chair was great—Keisha could see the

pond in the center of the golf course and tall stalks of
pink lilies growing along a fence.

Brookside really is a beautiful place, Keisha thought,
feeling glad all over again that she'd listened to Ellie
and gone up to the attic. For the first time since she'd
arrived at Brookside, she found herself thinking of Megan,
Alison, and Heather, and what had happened at the
drugstore. She couldn't remember a time when she'd felt
so different and apart from her best friends. Keisha
decided. But she still didn't know how to explain all her
feelings about being black to her friends.

Just then a mother and two small children carrying
dolphin-shaped floats unlatched the gate surrounding
the kiddie pool.

As Keisha turned to look at them, she saw Brandon
talking to Lisette outside the gate. Dylan was still in
his arms.

"So you will watch him for me?" Keisha heard
Brandon say.

"Sure," Lisette said, smoothing her long red ponytail.
"No problem."

No problem? Keisha shook her head in disbelief.
Of course it was a problem, she thought. Lisette was on
duty at the big pool all afternoon!

Chapter

Six

THE RESCUE

fter lunch, the lifeguards rotated assignments.
The large thermometer near the snack bar read
ninety degrees; it seemed as though everybody who
belonged to the country club was in the water, trying to
cool off. Keisha's end was crowded with kids swimming
and jumping in off the sides, and Morgan and another
lifeguard were giving swimming lessons to two groups of
small children. At the opposite end of the pool, a long line
of teenagers stood waiting to jump off the diving board.

"Hey, Lisette!" Keisha heard a girl call. "Want to come to the movies with us tonight?"

"No thanks," Lisette said. "We've got a lifeguard barbecue later."

Keisha shook her head. As usual, several kids were standing near Lisette's chair, talking and laughing with her. How can Lisette hang out with her friends *and* watch the pool? Keisha wondered. Obviously Lisette wasn't too worried about making sure the pool was well guarded.

Lisette didn't seem worried about watching Dylan either, Keisha realized. The little boy was sitting by himself in a lounge chair at the deep end, staring off into space. The poor little kid looked bored to tears.

A few minutes later, Keisha saw Dylan head toward the diving board. He reminded her a lot of her little brother, Ronnie, as he walked along the solid black line painted around the edge of the pool, carefully putting one foot down in front of the other.

Two little girls dashed past Keisha's chair. She jumped up and blew on her whistle. "No running near the pool."

The two girls immediately slowed down. "Sorry, Lifeguard," one of them said sheepishly.

Then Keisha had to blow the whistle at an older man who was wearing goggles and trying to swim laps in the shallow end. After pointing the man in the direction of the swimming lanes at the deep end of the pool, Keisha's eyes flicked back to where she'd seen last Dylan.

Maybe when I take my break, I'll go say hello to him, she thought. He seemed so lonely.

Her eyes traveled the length of the pool, trying to find the little boy. He must be with Lisette, she thought.

But to Keisha's surprise, Lisette's lifeguard chair was empty. Lisette was gone, too.

Keisha felt a spark of anger. Coach Owen had specifically told the lifeguards not to leave their chairs unless another guard was covering them. It was especially important to follow that rule on a busy day like today.

A nervous flutter had already started in Keisha's stomach when she heard a frightened shout ring out from alongside the pool.

"He can't swim!" a woman cried. "That little boy needs help!" She was pointing to a spot in the deep end, close to the diving boards.

Keisha's heart pounded in her chest as she realized that someone had fallen in, right near the section that Lisette was supposed to be guarding.

The rescue procedure that Coach Owen had explained

on the first day at Brookside reeled through Keisha's mind. She leaped up, frantically waving across the pool to Tyler.

"I'll go after him," she yelled. "You clear the pool." He nodded, then began blowing his whistle.

Keisha grabbed her rescue buoy, climbed down, and took off at a run. She kept her eyes trained on the spot where the woman had pointed. But she couldn't see anyone in the pool.

Suddenly a small dark head broke the surface of the water. Keisha gasped. It was Dylan!

A second later it disappeared.

Terrible, frightening thoughts whirled through Keisha's head. Dylan had been terrified of the water that morning at his swimming lesson. Now he was in water way over his head; the pool was at least twelve feet deep at that end.

Splash!

Keisha flung the rescue buoy into the water. Then she dove in, her arms stroking even before she came back up to the surface. She grabbed hold of the buoy and began swimming hard and fast toward the place where Dylan had disappeared.

What if I don't reach Dylan in time? What if I can't locate him? What if . . .

The terrible thoughts kept coming and coming.

When Keisha reached the center of the pool, she dove below the surface. Chlorine burned her eyes as she desperately scanned the depths of the pool.

Come on, Dylan, she thought. Where are you?

And then she found him.

Drifting toward the bottom of the pool was Dylan's limp body. He was unconscious.

Fear shot through Keisha like an electrical current. She couldn't let anything happen to him.

Her arms sliced through the water and her feet kicked furiously as she propelled herself toward him.

In seconds she was there.

Keisha wrapped one arm around the little boy. Using her other arm to swim, and kicking hard with her feet, she managed to pull him to the surface. Dimly, she saw a flash of blue sky and a blur of faces as she reached for the buoy and began to tow the boy across the pool.

You can do it, said a voice inside her head. You're almost there.

Keisha reached the side of the pool and grabbed hold. Tyler pulled the little boy out of the water. Keisha followed instantly. Her heart pounded wildly as she bent over the boy, lifeless on the concrete, and began CPR.

Just like Coach Owen had demonstrated, Keisha turned Dylan's face to the side, to make sure his mouth wasn't full of water. Then she turned him toward her again, tilted his head back, and pinched his nose shut. Placing her mouth over his to form a tight seal, she began to breathe into him. She watched his chest carefully, hoping to see it rise and fall, a sign that he was breathing.

But Dylan remained still. Keisha checked his pulse— there was none.

"I'll call an ambulance!" Tyler shouted frantically.

"You're doing great, Keisha," someone else urged her on. "Keep it up!"

Keisha had no idea who was talking to her. All she knew was that she had to start compressing Dylan's chest, to try to get his heart to beat again. She placed her hands in the right position on the little boy's breastbone and pumped down.

Seconds later, the miracle happened.

"He's breathing!" a woman shouted. "She did it! She saved the little boy!"

Keisha stopped for a second and looked at Dylan. His

chest was rising and falling, and when she checked his neck for a pulse, it was there.

Relief flooded over her. "You're okay, Dylan," she murmured. You're going to be okay."

The next few minutes were a total blur to Keisha. Coach Owen burst through the crowd, followed by Brandon and the boy's mother. A member of the club who was a doctor rushed over and checked Dylan carefully. Keisha thought she heard an ambulance's siren in the distance.

As the others took over, Keisha staggered to her feet. Her legs felt like rubber as she made her way over to a lounge chair and sat down.

Lisette hurried toward her, looking pale and worried. "Great job, Keisha," she began. "I knew you—"

Suddenly all the fear and anger Keisha had been holding back boiled up inside her. "Where were you, Lisette?" Keisha shouted, barely recognizing her own voice. "You were supposed to be on duty!"

"Calm down, Keisha." Lisette laughed nervously. "Dylan's fine."

"You had no right saying you'd watch Dylan when you were on duty," Keisha went on, "and you had no right leaving your chair. That's why you didn't even see Dylan fall in."

Lisette flushed. "Lighten up, will you?" she said, shaking her head as if she couldn't believe how crazy Keisha was acting.

"I won't lighten up, Lisette!" Keisha shot back. "I'm sick and tired of watching you treat Morgan like she doesn't belong here, when you're the one who doesn't belong on the lifeguard squad!" Tears streamed down her cheeks. "Dylan could have drowned, you know!"

Then another voice chimed in.

"She's right, Lisette," Coach Owen said sternly. "Dylan nearly drowned. And I want to see you in my office—now!"

Chapter
Seven

GOING HOME

he sun was beginning to set over the golf course. All the swimmers had gone home, and the bustling country club seemed still and lifeless. The only people left were the squad of lifeguards, who were gathered around the pool for a special meeting called by Coach Owen.

Keisha took a seat at one of the picnic

tables. The lifeguards were quiet and somber. For once nobody was laughing or fooling around.

"I called this meeting so that we could talk about what happened at the pool today," the coach said. "As all of you know, Keisha and Tyler saved a little boy's life, and I'm really proud of them. They did exactly what they were supposed to do."

"Way to go, Keisha and Tyler," called out one of the older lifeguards.

"You guys were great," Morgan added. She gave Keisha a warm smile.

"So do we get a reward or something?" Tyler joked.

For the first time, everyone laughed.

"My praise," Coach Owen answered. "Along with Dylan's parents' deepest thanks."

"That's good enough," Tyler said in a more serious tone. "We're just glad that Dylan's okay."

Keisha nodded.

"I also wanted to let the squad know that Lisette has been placed on two weeks probation," Coach Owen went on. "This means that she won't be guarding the pool, and she won't be allowed to attend any lifeguard functions, like tonight's barbecue."

Keisha glanced over at Lisette, who was sitting by herself on one of the lounges. She was looking down as

she closely examined a strand of her long red hair.

"I hope that what happened today serves as a reminder that lifeguarding is a big responsibility," Coach Owen said. "As the word says, we guard lives." She glanced over at Keisha. "Great job," she repeated softly. Then her face relaxed. "Now let's have some fun. The barbecue starts in ten minutes."

As the meeting broke up, Keisha heard someone call out her name. It was Lisette, who was hurrying toward her.

As she approached, Lisette flashed Keisha a smile. "I

meant what I said before," she murmured. "You did a great job today. If it weren't for you . . ." She looked down, without finishing her sentence. Still, Keisha understood what she was trying to say. In spite of everything, Lisette was very relieved that Keisha had been there to rescue Dylan.

"Thanks," Keisha said. "It sounds like the coach was pretty fair with you—two weeks probation isn't so bad."

"I guess." Lisette shrugged as she smoothed out her long red hair. "I mean, I know I made a big mistake, but I have to admit I'm pretty disappointed about missing out on everything. Especially the barbecue."

Keisha was surprised to feel a sudden twinge of pity for Lisette. It must be hard for her to deal with being on probation, she thought. And even harder for her to deal with the fact that Dylan had nearly drowned—all because of her.

Keisha nodded. "It's never easy to be left out of things," she said sympathetically. Then something occurred to her. "But maybe it will help you to understand how Morgan feels when you leave her out," she added softly.

Lisette looked surprised. "I don't think you understand, Keisha," she said in a cold tone. "My parents are members of Brookside because they want me to hang out with the right kind of people. And frankly, Morgan just isn't that kind of person."

Inside, Keisha fumed. Every ounce of pity she'd felt for Lisette had evaporated. "Well, that's a shame," she said as evenly as she could. "Because everybody else at Brookside likes Morgan a lot. In fact, none of the other lifeguards care one bit about what her father does or how much money her family has."

A small smile crept across Lisette's face as she stood there looking at Keisha. "See you around," was all she said as she wiggled her fingers in a little wave and strode off toward the parking lot.

Keisha sighed as she watched Lisette climb into her mother's sleek yellow car. Oh well, she consoled herself, at least I told her what I thought.

A moment later, Keisha forgot all about Lisette Wilson. As Tyler rushed by, carrying several cans of soda, he nudged her gently with his elbow. "Hey, Keisha, it's party time!"

Keisha smiled as the deserted country club suddenly filled once again with the sounds of people having fun. Rock music blared from two speakers set up on the patio, and several lifeguards dove into the pool and started tossing a beach ball back and forth. The coach had rolled out a grill and was cooking hot dogs and hamburgers.

"I bet you're ready for dinner," someone said from behind Keisha.

It was Morgan.

Keisha grinned. "How did you know I'm starved?"

"Rescuing people is hard work," Morgan teased her. She pointed to a table with a white umbrella. "I'm sitting over there with Tyler and a couple of other kids. Why don't you grab some food and join us?"

"That sounds like fun," Keisha replied. "Thanks. I'll be there in a minute."

But as Keisha stood on line waiting for a hot dog, she changed her mind. Suddenly all she wanted was to go back to Ellie's, where she knew another dinner and a good friend were waiting.

With one last look at the sun going down over the golf course, and the clear blue pool shimmering in the dusk, Keisha turned around and headed for the locker room.

Before she looked into the mirror that would send her on her way home, she reached into her beach bag. There was something that she wanted to leave behind at Brookside.

Eight

BEST FRIENDS FOREVER

 hat is so amazing, Keisha," Heather exclaimed. "You actually saved a little boy's life!"

"You're a true hero, Keisha," Megan added.

"Thanks." Keisha smiled shyly as her friends congratulated her. She didn't usually feel shy around Alison, Megan, and Heather, but this was the first time she'd seen them since the incident at the pharmacy.

That afternoon the four of them were hanging out in Alison's room, talking about Keisha's adventure at Brookside Country Club.

"Morgan sounds nice," Alison remarked. "I hope Lisette does start to treat her better."

"Me, too," Keisha said. "But I doubt it. I have a feeling that Lisette and her parents are always going to look down on Morgan because her family's not wealthy."

"That's the most ridiculous thing I've ever heard," Heather said indignantly. "People can be so snobbish sometimes."

"That reminds me," Megan said suddenly, looking at Keisha. "Ellie told me that you've decided to go back to Mr. Burns's store tomorrow."

Keisha nodded as she glanced over at her friends. The three of them were all watching Keisha nervously, as if they didn't quite know what to expect from her.

"What are you going to tell him?" Heather asked.

Alison put it more bluntly. "How do you tell somebody that they acted like a major jerk?" she said, screwing up her face.

At that they all giggled.

Keisha felt the mood in the room lighten. "I haven't figured out exactly what I'm going to say," she said truthfully. "But I think I'm going to try to tell Mr. Burns that what he did is wrong. It's not right to judge people by

how they look. Or by how old they are. Or by—"

"How much money they have," Heather chimed in.

Keisha nodded.

"Would it be okay if we came with you, Keisha?" Megan asked. "The way Mr. Burns treated you really bothered me, too."

Alison shook her head in agreement.

Keisha looked at her friends. "Do you really want to come?" she asked.

"Absolutely," Heather answered for all of them.

Keisha smiled. "I think I'll feel a lot braver with you guys there," she admitted. "Let's go right after school."

Maybe it doesn't matter if Alison, Heather, and Megan don't understand everything about me, Keisha realized. The important thing is that they care about me, and try to understand my feelings, and that they aren't about to judge me by the color of my skin. That's what I do with them, too, Keisha thought. I try to understand, even if I don't know anything about speed skating, or about being Jewish like Heather, or about having divorced parents like Megan.

"Okay, you guys." Alison suddenly jumped off her bed, interrupting Keisha's thoughts. "I'm going downstairs to grab a snack. What should I bring us?"

"Potato chips!"

"Popcorn!"

"Chocolate chip cookies!"

Keisha, Heather, and Megan called out all at once.

Alison laughed. "Uh-oh," she said. "I was thinking about pretzels!"

At that they *all* started laughing.

Diary

Dear Diary:

I did it! My friends and I went to Mr. Burns's store, and I told him exactly what I thought—that he should get to know me before he decides what kind of person I am. When I was finished talking to him, he just stood there, staring at me, as if I were an alien from outer space. I think I gave him the biggest shock of his life. And you know what? It felt great! Maybe the next time an African-American person goes into his store, he won't automatically assume she's going to steal something.

I'm still thinking about how cool it was to be a lifeguard at Brookside Country Club. I was really scared when Dylan fell in the pool and nearly drowned. Luckily, I was paying attention to Coach Owen. Just like she said, CPR really can save lives.

I hope Morgan found the present I left in her locker. I didn't need the swimsuit anymore, and I was pretty sure that Ellie wouldn't mind if I gave it away. I was right—she was thrilled to hear that I left the suit for Morgan.

I'll write again soon!

Keisha